1 • 2 • 3
Valentine's Day

1 • 2 • 3
Valentine's Day

by Jeanne Modesitt
Illustrated by Robin Spowart

Boyds Mills Press

Published by Caroline House
Boyds Mills Press, Inc.
A Highlights Company
815 Church Street
Honesdale, Pennsylvania 18431
Printed in China
Visit our website at: www.boydsmillspress.com

U.S. Cataloging-in-Publication Data
(Library of Congress Standards)

Modesitt, Jeanne.
One, two, three, Valentine's Day / by Jeanne Modesitt ; illustrated by
Robin Spowart.— 1st ed.
[32] p. : col. ill. ;   cm.
Summary : Mister Mouse delivers Valentine gifts to his friends in this
counting picture book that includes a Valentine activity.
ISBN   1-56397-868-7
1. Valentine's Day — Juvenile fiction. 2. Counting — Juvenile literature.
[1.
Valentine's Day — Fiction. 2. Counting.] I. Spowart, Robin. II. Title.
[E]   21   2002   CIP
2001086385

First edition, 2002
The text of this book is set in 22-point Serif Gothic.

10 9 8 7 6 5 4 3 2 1

To our little sweetheart, Katie
J.M. and R.S.

Mister Mouse with the big red box
Goes up to the door and gives two knocks.
ONE little frog with a big bow tie
Opens the door and gets a pink pie.
"Happy Valentine's!" says Mister Mouse,
And off he goes to another house.

1

Mister Mouse with the big red box
Goes up to the door and gives two knocks.
TWO round pigs, dressed oh-so-dandy,
Open the door and get some candy.
"Happy Valentine's!" says Mister Mouse,
And off he goes to another house.

1   2

Mister Mouse with the big red box
Goes up to the door and gives two knocks.
THREE big badgers, whistling a tune,
Open the door and get a balloon.
"Happy Valentine's!" says Mister Mouse,
And off he goes to another house.

Mister Mouse with the big red box
Goes up to the door and gives two knocks.
FOUR tiny hens with four tiny combs
Open the door and get some poems.
"Happy Valentine's!" says Mister Mouse,
And off he goes to another house.

1 2 3 4

Mister Mouse with the big red box
Goes up to the door and gives two knocks.
FIVE spotted dogs, their tails wagging hard,
Open the door and get a big card.
"Happy Valentine's!" says Mister Mouse,
And off he goes to another house.

1   2   3   4   5

Mister Mouse with the big red box
Goes up to the door and gives two knocks.
SIX merry ducks, their eyes so bright,
Open the door and get a red kite.
"Happy Valentine's!" says Mister Mouse,
And off he goes to another house.

1   2   3   4   5   6

Mister Mouse with the big red box
Goes up to the door and gives two knocks.
SEVEN white cats, ribbons in their hair,
Open the door and get a teddy bear.
"Happy Valentine's!" says Mister Mouse,
And off he goes to another house.

1 2 3 4 5 6 7

Mister Mouse with the big red box
Goes up to the door and gives two knocks.
EIGHT small moles (whom you couldn't tell apart)
Open the door and get a red heart.
"Happy Valentine's!" says Mister Mouse,
And off he goes to another house.

1   2   3   4   5   6   7   8

Mister Mouse with the big red box
Goes up to the door and gives two knocks.
NINE brown bunnies with twitching noses
Open the door and get some roses.
"Happy Valentine's!" says Mister Mouse,
And off he goes to another house.

1   2   3   4   5   6   7   8   9

Mister Mouse with the big red box
Goes up to the door and gives two knocks.
TEN little mice, so happy and glad,
Open the door and get toys from Dad.
"Happy Valentine's!" says Mister Mouse,
And inside he goes, into his house!

1 2 3 4 5 6 7 8 9 10

How to Make a **Valentine's Day Heart**

This is a very special heart that you can hang up. Have fun!

You will need:
  White paper
  Pencil
  Scissors
  Red construction paper
  String
  Tape

2. Cut along the line you drew.

1. Take a piece of white paper and fold it in half. Draw the shape of half of a heart.

3. Unfold the paper, which is now in the shape of a heart.

4. Put your heart shape on top of the red construction paper. Hold the heart shape down with one hand, and with your other hand, draw around the outside of the heart with a pencil.

5. Cut out the heart shape that you have drawn on the red construction paper.

6. Take your string and cut off a small piece. Tape one end of the small piece of string on one side of the red heart, then tape the other end of the small string on the other side of the red heart.

7. Now it's time to decorate! On your red heart you can write: I Love You or Be My Valentine. Glue something pretty, like glitter, buttons, or candy hearts, or draw little hearts. Invent something of you own!

Happy Valentine's Day